Published by Modern Publishing
A Division of Unisystems, Inc.

Printed in Singapore

DOGGONE DAYS™
Flops in Space

by Eve Rose

MODERN PUBLISHING
A Division of Unisystems, Inc.
New York, New York 10022

One day, after school, Adam and I went into the basement.

"Look, Flops," he said to me. "This is a drawing of the rocket ship I'm going to build for my science fair project."

"It's a galaxy explorer. I hope it wins
first prize. You can help me make it," Adam said.

Adam and I carried some old furniture and things upstairs and into the backyard.

We hammered and nailed and glued
all afternoon.
"It's done," said Adam. "Now let's
climb on and fly through space!"
FLY? That sounded kind of scary.
"Don't worry," Adam said. "It will be fun.
I'll be the captain, and you'll be my first mate."

First Mate Flops. Hmm . . . I liked that.

"Here is your space helmet, First Mate," Captain Adam said. "Let's climb aboard and prepare for take-off."

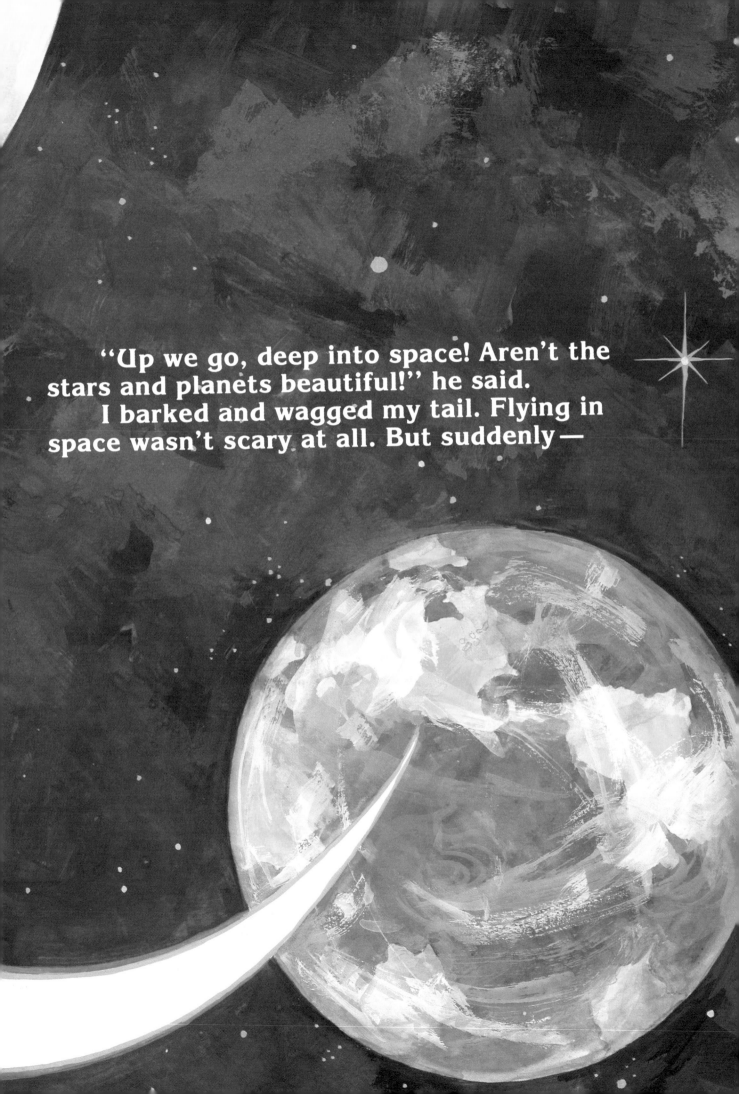

"Up we go, deep into space! Aren't the stars and planets beautiful!" he said.
I barked and wagged my tail. Flying in space wasn't scary at all. But suddenly—

"Meteors coming in from all sides!"
shouted Adam. "Raise the shields,
First Mate Flops!"
    I looked over my shoulder and saw
a strange spaceship. It was headed
right for us!

"Grrrrufff!" I yelped in warning. Adam made a sharp turn. "We'll have to land on that orange planet over there," he said. "We need to get more fuel and check our rocket for damage."

It sounded like a good idea, but just before we landed, we saw a huge space creature waving at us.

"Stop growling, Flops," Adam said to me. "Maybe he's a friendly space creature."

"Hello," said the creature. "I've brought you some good things to eat."

"Space food!" smiled Adam. "I'm sure it will be tasty."

I sniffed at my bowl, and then took a bite. Whatever it was, it was delicious.

After we ate, we checked the rocket and Adam put more fuel in the tank.

"We'd better get back to earth now," said Adam. "I'll bring the rocket home after the fair tomorrow and we can fly again."

The next day, I couldn't wait for Adam
to get home. When he finally walked through
the door, he looked very sad.

"I didn't win a prize, Flops," he whispered
in my ear. "And everyone laughed at my rocket.
They said it was nothing but a bunch of
old furniture."

Old furniture? Our galaxy explorer?
Nonsense! I barked, and wagged my tail, and
licked Adam's face over and over until he smiled.
     Then I pulled him out to the yard where
the rocket ship lay waiting.
     "Okay, First Mate Flops," Adam laughed.
"Get ready for blast off. We're going to Mars!"

And we did.